MW01047453

This book belongs to:

_____

I dedicate this book to my two sons Derrion and Jaleel. May you always have the courage to put God first, be true to yourself, be great at whatever you put your mind to, and love what you enjoy doing. You are someone! Never let anyone make you feel you are not capable or great enough to do better or achieve more. Your ideas matter but your actions matter more. Give life your very best and watch the future explode brighter with bigger and better for you!

Love, Mom & Dad

My Favorite Future

Written by
Portia Bright Pittman

Illustrated by
Harry Aveira

Dear Reader,

One day, I watched my first son Derrion explore around the house. I began imagining what he would become if only he put his mind to it as he traveled through his youthful years as a kid. This book is meant for you.

Take a moment while reading to envision what you want to be and have the courage to pursue it. Life is a journey not a marathon. Never shy away from the work that it takes to become the greatest version of yourself. You are somebody great and something great is inside of you.

Sincerely Yours,

Portia Bright Pittman

My favorite future explorer...

has already conquered his first steps.
Where will he go next?

My favorite future drummer...

is dismantling his drum set. He imagines himself building the biggest drum set ever.

My favorite future football star...

is already practicing gripping, throwing, and holding a football. Soon he will take the ball over the finish line.

My favorite future DJ...

is making music on the piano from his highchair at the dinner table. His parents can already feel the beat.

My favorite future computer scientist...

is already touching Mommy and Daddy's computer. One day he will have his own computer and will teach children how to use it.

My favorite future chef...

is already sampling pizza sauce. When he is older, he will cook meals for people around world.

My favorite future pastor...

is in the living room listening to gospel music and dancing with Grandma. One day he will be doing his own sermon in church while Grandma dances in the pews.

My favorite future engineer...

is already working on his first robot. When he grows up, he will create robots that can do many different things.

My favorite future barber...

is learning to brush his wild, curly hair with Daddy's brush. One day he will be combing, brushing, and cutting hair for others.

My favorite future NBA player...

is bouncing the ball, dreaming of his first shot. One day he will make the best drop shot.

My favorite future astronaut...

is viewing images of space through Daddy's telescope. One day he will be traveling through outer space on a giant spaceship.

My favorite future
is loving on me!

I tell him what I have learned from experience...
there is no limit to what you can become!

About the Author

Portia served as legislative assistant for legislators in the North Carolina Senate and House of Representatives. She expresses her passion for youth by helping them understand how government works. Portia leads programs for schools, faith communities, and civic groups about the legislative process. Contact her at brightbooks.org for details.

Take your imagination to our coloring and activity book sold separately.

The activity book has coloring pages and positive affirmations to empower youth.

Please continue to follow the journey by subscribing to our youtube channel, facebook, instragram and tiktok @brightbooksclub

Visit our website at www.brightbooks.org

Made in the USA
Columbia, SC
25 July 2024

38737785R00018